Midnight The Witching Hour

Sharon Barnes

S&D Publishing

Copyright © 2024 by Sharon Barnes

All rights reserved. No part of this text may be used or reproduced in any manner whatsoever without the express written permission of the publisher and/or the author, except in the case of brief quotations embodied in critical articles and reviews.

No part of this book may be used in any manner for purposes of training artificial intelligence (AI) to generate audio or text, including without limitation, technologies that are capable of generating works in the same genre as this work without the specific and express permission of the author.

Author's reassurance to the readers:
NO artificial intelligence (AI) was used in the
development/writing/editing/proofing/formatting/publication of this novel.

Edits were completed by several individuals. We have tried to make this book the best it can be. I do apologize if there are any typos or grammatical errors, we are human after all and no one is perfect.

This is a work of fiction. Names, characters, places, and incidents are either the product of the author's imagination or are used fictitiously. Any resemblance to actual persons, living or dead, business establishments, events, or locales is entirely coincidental.

Cover and Illustrations by Chris Ross

Print ISBN-13: 979-8-9918869-1-8
eBook ISBN-13: 979-8-9918869-0-1

Published by S&D Publishing
sharonabarnes.com

To all those out there that have been made to believe or feel that they are not good enough... just know, you are someone special and can accomplish great things. Believe in yourself!

Sharon Barnes

To Daniel, Hermione, Bryant, and Justice— Thank you for loving me with all my crazy quirks and papers everywhere. To all my friends and fellow writers of Writer's Round Table, thank you for all the critiques and support over the years. Eric, thank you for your friendship, support, and encouragement on this adventure.

"Magic comes from what is inside you. It is a part of you. You can't weave together a spell you don't believe in."

Jim Butcher

The Protector's Return

Slow soulful jazz was playing on the record player. The wine glass was sitting half empty on the coffee table. Exhaustion had engulfed Liz; she couldn't fight it any longer. She had turned on the jazz and had a glass of wine knowing they would relax her. The nightmares had started again. Caffeine of any form had become her drug of choice, to ensure she could stay awake and keep the horrible dreams at bay. Exhaustion and the jitters overwhelmed her to the point she was not functioning at her best. She needed the slow rhythmic peace of jazz. It would help her mind to relax.

The jazz lulled her to sweet blissful dreams, but then the clock tower struck twelve midnight. Her eyes popped open. *No.* She thought. *I can't move again. This is my home.* She stood and walked over to the old farmhouse window. She felt a cool draft and wrapped her arms around herself. He was there, she could see his outline. She sighed. It had been twenty years since she had seen that profile, but it was still the same. He stood six feet two inches, weighing approximately one hundred ninety pounds and was dressed in solid black with a long black leather duster. His hat was a leather-looking cowboy hat, however, it had a round brim, similar to gamblers hat. He was smoking a cigar.

That was ironic since half his face had been burned and scarred in a house fire twenty years ago. It must be bad for him to pick up that habit. He was her protector. She knew he was always around however she didn't typically see him. When she did see him it meant things were going bad fast. She grabbed her cloak and slipped into a pair of worn clogs that were by the back door. She didn't speak until she was directly beside him. She lived on two hundred acres of land and her home sat way back in from the road and any neighbors, but tonight it felt like there were eyes on them, watching. The conversation needed to be only heard by them.

"Liz."

"How bad is it?"

"May I come in for a shot of whiskey?"

"That bad?"

He gave a slight nod. She knew her feelings of being watched were confirmed when he asked to come in. If he wanted to be in the house he could have been without permission. By asking, he was letting her know that no one needed to enter her home from this moment forward except for her and him, unless permission was granted. Permission did not come easily.

Liz was a self-sufficient woman that could do any essential tasks, such as plumbing, electrical work, and anything in between if needed. She learned quickly not to trust people completely. She had friends, but they always met in public and never at her home. She didn't want it to ever slip out where she lived if any of her friends were ever asked. She was protected, however so were they. They couldn't be forced to release information if they didn't know it. It was a lonely life, but for the most part, Liz preferred it.

The protector entered the house after Liz. He quickly shut the door and bolted it. He removed his black boots and quietly walked to the living room. Liz was too anxious to sit. She walked back into the kitchen and started a pot of coffee. He was still standing when she walked back into the living room. The smoke from his cigar clung to his clothes. It was a sweet clove smell. He had put out the cigar before he entered her house. She despised people smoking inside houses and restaurants. There were too many horrible memories attached to cigarettes and houses. It had cost her not only her childhood home, but one of her foster homes and much more. A shiver ran from the base of her spine all the way to the top of her scalp.

"Tell me Lucas."

"In time, but now you must sleep. All is well, I am here."

How in the world am I supposed to sleep? She thought.

He walked in her room, opened her top drawer, and pulled out a pair of thick fuzzy socks. He quickly went to the kitchen to start the kettle. He knew she preferred coffee, however she needed the relaxation of his tea. He walked back into the living room, sat her down, took the coffee cup from her hands and placed the socks on her feet. She didn't question how he knew where her socks were, he knew almost everything about her, he had been with her since the day that she was born. Knowing where she kept her socks had not changed since she was four.

She heard the tea kettle whistle and then he returned with a steaming cup of tea. It smelled a lot like sleepy time tea, but she knew that it was one of his special blends that he made himself. She relaxed just by the smell of the tea and his presence. She felt the exhaustion taking hold to pull her into a deep sleep. She drank the tea while it was still hot and laid down on the couch. Warmth embraced her.

Revelations

The room was so warm. A fire must be going in the fireplace. She slowly was coming around; the warmth felt so good. It must be about to snow if Lucas had built a fire. She stretched and bumped into something. She opened her eyes and realized it was Lucas. He was sitting on the couch with her head in his lap.

"How long have the dreams been back, Liz?"

"A week or two."

"You should have called."

"I didn't want to bother you."

He laughed a deep raspy laugh. "A bother? Hmmm, I think that falls under my job description as a protector. Don't you think?"

"You have already done so much," Liz said.

Lucas shook his head. Liz had always been independent, even when she was five and he had to quickly get her to safety. She was determined to protect him. The memory made him chuckle. The first fifteen years of her life had been grueling; thankfully, she has had twenty years of peace. They both knew the dreams were more than dreams or nightmares, they were warnings. He stood and walked over to the fireplace. "They found your brother."

Her heart sank. The memories flooded her with those words. Her parents had been killed two days after her brother had been born.

Liz had grabbed him and ran to the cellar when the intruders had entered. She could hear her mother's deafening screams and the blows being thrown. The noise wouldn't stop, and she couldn't tune it out no matter how hard she tried. That night had haunted her for years.

The smoke came when things finally fell silent. Fear gripped her chest she couldn't lose Zachary too. No one had to tell her that her parents were dead, she knew. That was when Lucas appeared. She thought he was the Grim Reaper because he was in black, but he didn't scare her.

"I'm Liz. We have to go, sir. If you can get me to the door then I can get us out.'

"Liz, can I have Zachary?"

"No!" She stood tall with complete determination of a five-year-old girl.

"I promise once we are outside, I will give him back to you."

"No Mister."

He shook his head and picked her up while she held Zachary. Once outside he sat her down. She grabbed his hand and pulled him to the shadows. "Are you the Grim Reaper?"

"No. I'm Lucas your protector."

She studied him for a moment. "Ok. Come with me before the bad people come back. I'll protect you."

He smiled. "I think that is my job."

She shrugged and led him to her special place. Her parents had trained her well and they prepared for this day. Clothes for both children, a small number of toys, and preserved food, enough for a few years, water, formula, and bottles lined the shelves.

The hidey-hole was underground, but barely. The backside led to a cave. It was near a stream so she could bathe and get water, but it would also mask their sounds and their scents. Lucas was pleased that they would be safe for a night or two. He wouldn't risk anything longer than that. He was worried about telling her that Zachary wouldn't be with them on the next part of their journey. Liz watched his expression darken.

"Mr. Lucas, you look hungry. Please sit so I can get us all some food. Can you please hold Zachary?"

He had smiled and gladly accepted the baby. Zachary had not cried once.

Liz spun around. "Don't try to leave."

"I wouldn't."

"Good."

She quickly got a stale loaf of bread, a jar of peanut butter and jelly. She made herself a sandwich and Mr. Lucas two sandwiches. She pulled out a jar of homemade pickles and some salted roasted peanuts; they were her father's specialty. She carried Mr. Lucas his sandwiches, went back to the makeshift counter to get the pickles and peanuts, and finally her sandwich. She got two mason jars for water. She quietly slipped out and walked out to the stream. Lucas was on his feet and quickly followed her. He would not lose her; she was his responsibility. She turned and smiled. She said nothing.

Zachary's eyes were open. Lucas looked at him. Zachary was the quietest baby he had ever seen. She filled the glasses and made her way back inside. She sat the glasses down on the table. She grabbed a basket that was lined with rabbit furs and pulled it where she could see it from the table. She walked over to Lucas and held out her hands, but he took her hand and carried Zachary to the basket. She watched carefully to make sure he didn't drop her baby brother. Once he was laid down, Liz ran to get him a bottle. She made the bottle, exactly the way her Mama had shown her. Lucas watched as she did every task with precision. She was too young to have to deal with this. The Blackthornes didn't care how old she or her brother were, they would kill them regardless of their age. He shook his head. Liz fed Zachary his bottle.

Finally, she sat down to eat. Lucas waited until she sat down before he took a bite of his food. He thanked her for the wonderful dinner. That was the first night that she truly felt safe. She loved her parents, but there was always an embedded fear that they would have to flee at any moment. Her mother worried the whole time she was pregnant. Her father delivered Zachary at home because of her fear of going to the hospital. Liz yawned wide. It had been a long day.

Lucas pulled out a couple of deer hides and a bear fur and made Liz a nice soft pallet. He gathered a couple blankets and tucked her in. He gently got Zachary out of his basket, burped, and changed him. He held Zachary until he went back to sleep. He stood guard all night. The next day Liz packed Zachary's bag and basket.

She took Lucas's hand and said, "Morning Star waits." Lucas just looked at her, he had not said anything to her about the next part of their journey.

That's interesting. I wonder if she is a seer. It would make sense since her grandmother was such a powerful witch.

He smiled, "yes, she is waiting. Are you ok?" She simply nodded.

She sat up straighter. She let the memories pass. She was thankful that Lucas had allowed her to handle those memories as they had engulfed her. She wiped a tear from her cheek.

"Is he dead?" Her voice cracked as she asked him.

"No."

"No?" Liz asked in shock.

He shook his head. "Zachary didn't know anything. All he knows is that he's Morning Star's son. They only sensed his native trainings."

"And Morning Star?"

"Too stubborn to die."

She didn't like that answer. "Lucas, please tell me."

"She was tortured, but never talked. They let her live as a reminder to the locals."

"How old is she, like sixty years old?'

"Seventy-two."

"And they tortured her?"

He gave a curt nod. Liz stood and stormed into the kitchen. Once in the kitchen she screamed at the empty room, releasing her frustration and cried. She sat down hard in her kitchen chair and just let the tears fall. Lucas could hear her crying, but he waited because he knew she needed to think. She needed a glass of wine. She poured herself a glass, took a long sip, poured Lucas a glass and then carried both glasses into the living room. He accepted the glass, but he didn't drink it. Instead, he sat it on the mantel and took her hand.

Confessions

The sweet clove smell engulfed Liz's senses. She inhaled deeply to fully take in his scent and embrace the comfort and security of having him nearby.

"Relax," he said.

"I can't."

He gently pulled her close. He wouldn't ever overstep his bounds with her. He hugged her. She felt warm and safe in his embrace. He stroked her back in a comforting manner. She had thoughts that she knew had to be forbidden, but she didn't push them away, not this time. She had fought those feelings for too long. She nuzzled closer to his chest. Lucas took a deep breath, inhaling the smell of her shampoo. *This is new. In the past she would barely hug me.* His thoughts were drifting. He made sure that he was in the here and now. He wrapped his arms around her pulling her closer. He just held her for several minutes before he spoke.

"Liz, what are you thinking?"

"You don't want to know."

"If I didn't, then I wouldn't have asked."

She took a deep breath, taking in his scent again. She eased the breath out as a means to ease her nerves. "Are we forbidden?"

"Forbidden? What do you mean?"

"From being as one?"

He stood there holding her. He gently raised her chin so he could look in her eyes. "Is that what you want?"

"You have no idea. I've wanted that for years."

He took her glass of wine and sat it on the mantle.

"Lizwyna Clay Krimshaw, may I kiss you?"

"Yes please."

He kissed her and the temperature in the room went up about ten degrees. He picked her up so that her legs were straddling his waist.

"Are you absolutely sure?"

"Yes."

Her protector showed her an amazing night. She realized he had never answered her.

"Lucas is this forbidden?" she asked again.

"No, not as long as I don't push the relationship or get upset when you date others."

She kissed him. The thought of dating others made her laugh. She couldn't remember the last time she had dated. She thought between his kisses and his touch. She remembered the last guy she dated was a complete jerk. He was nice when they were alone, but when they were out with people, he had an air of control about him. No thank you.

"I don't see that as an issue," she said.

"Liz, we have work to do. They have found Zachary, and I don't need them finding you."

"They know where I am."

Lucas bolted out of the bed and threw his clothes on.

"Let's go."

"No. This is my home, and I refuse to lose it."

"Unless you have tapped into your heritage and embraced it then I would advise you to grab your things and let's go."

She got up slowly, threw on her nightgown, kissed him, and walked into the kitchen. She made a pot of coffee. He walked in behind her with a hint of annoyance.

"Lucas, I have made this my home for twenty years. I don't have friends over for fear that they might be asked to talk, knowing they wouldn't be as strong as Morning Star. I have also never forgotten my heritage. Please sit and have a cup of coffee."

"We have work to do."

"Yes, we do, but coffee first."

He sat at the table and watched as she prepared the coffee. She was at ease even with the knowledge that they were coming. He had watched over her since she was born, he had not seen signs of her practicing. She seemed like the young five-year-old with determination that he rescued so long ago. He stood abruptly and went into the living room where he had left his duster. The package was small, hopefully she would like it. When he returned to the kitchen, he walked behind her and gently pulled her hair back. He saw the scar and gently traced it. He blamed himself for that scar as well as many others. If she hadn't been such a fighter, they would both be dead.

She turned, "Lucas, those scars are not your fault, now wash away that guilt."

"I should have arrived sooner."

"If I remember correctly, you were bleeding badly when you arrived."

Lucas bit his lip. "Happy Birthday."

He placed a necklace around her neck. It was a hand carved buffalo on a black leather strap. She ran her hand over the buffalo, feeling every detail. She brought it to her mouth and kissed it.

"Thank you." She said calmly, turned, went to the fridge, and gathered items for their breakfast.

"Do you not like it?" Lucas asked.

He had expected a little more reaction from her. This was the first time he was able to actually give her a birthday present in person. In the past he simply left them on the porch or in front of the door.

"Of course, I love it. Thank you."

Lucas walked up behind her and kissed her neck. "What? Do you regret us?"

"No, not at all."

"Well?"

"I'm thinking," Liz said.

"About?"

"Righting old wrongs."

Lucas wasn't sure what she had in mind. He also knew she didn't lie, no matter what the cost was to herself, she was honest to a fault. He fell in beside her to help with breakfast. They had an unspoken rhythm to their movements. It was a well-choreographed dance that was unrehearsed.

He took the glasses from the cupboard and poured them each a small glass of orange juice. He admired the cupboards and the craftsmanship. When he brought Liz here twenty years ago, it was a sturdy home, but it needed a lot of noticeable repairs, He had ripped out the floors and repaired them as well as the front porch and steps, but he had to leave after two weeks. The rest had been left for her to finish.

Every year on her birthday he would leave a present on her back stoop. He noticed all the changes from outside. He had no need to enter until yesterday. He hadn't wanted to cause her any unnecessary worry. Her life had been too hard as it was.

After breakfast she immediately began cleaning her tidy simple kitchen. She only owned the basics and most of those were handmade. Her table was varnished a green color with four chairs. It sat in the center of the room. She had cast iron skillets hanging on the wall, there

MIDNIGHT THE WITCHING HOUR   13

were four of those. There was no dishwasher because she preferred to wash everything by hand.

The water was scalding hot, he could tell by how red her hands were every time she pulled them out of the water. He took her soapy hand and gently pulled her over to him. He took a towel off of the counter, wiped her hand free of suds, and led her to the living room. He changed the record to BB King and danced with her for two songs. She touched his face and kissed him.

"Thank you for the present."

"You are welcome."

"Will Zachary come looking for me?"

He shook his head. "Morning Star has a great deal of healing to do. His only concern is to help her heal."

She nodded. She had been lonely over the years and had wondered what it would be like to have family close but pushed those thoughts away as quickly as they had arrived.

"Lucas, why didn't you ever knock or come in?"

"I didn't want to cause you worry. Seeing me is just like the dreams, a warning that the bad is closing in."

She shook her head. "It is actually the exact opposite. You always bring me peace."

He was speechless. After the second song she went back to the kitchen to finish her chore. He stood in the living room for a minute to absorb what she had said. He had watched her from a distance with every man she dated. Once she even came close to dating a young Blackthorne, but they didn't for one reason or another. A friend had introduced them at a local bar. He had asked her out, but the day they were to meet he canceled. She had not known that he was a Blackthorne because his last name was Meadow, but rest assured Lucas knew he was a cousin twice removed. If they had gone out, he would have guessed who she was. The young distant relatives thought of the Blackthorne and Krimshaw squabbles as a modern-day Romeo and

Juliet, but it was so much more than that. There was nothing to be romanticized in this family feud. Jealousy yes, but not romance.

He removed the wine glasses from the mantel and carried them to the kitchen to be washed. Liz finished the dishes and wiped down the counters, table, and stove. She went to her room to get dressed. When she walked out Lucas stood.

"What the hell are you wearing?"

"Clothes," she said with a lot of attitude.

She was wearing a blue and green plaid long sleeve shirt; blue jeans and her raven black hair was pulled back into a ponytail.

"It's Saturday, I'm off and I am going to feed the chickens. Plus, I'm going out to my studio, I need to replenish several of the local boutiques."

He stepped in her path. "We have work to do."

"So work, I'm not running."

He touched her shoulder and could feel the scar through her shirt.

"This time they will not leave any stones untouched."

"Let them."

"NO!" He bellowed.

The room became very warm from his anger. She simply touched his cheek, and his temper subsided. She took his hand and led him to the attic. He stood in a room filled with maps, candles, and papers posted beside certain maps. He ran his hand over the first map, it hummed at his touch. He turned to face her.

"I never stopped practicing the craft. Not when I was five, ten, fifteen, or now. Why do you think my first foster parents beat me?"

The left corner of his mouth tightened, and his jaw flexed in anger. He hated to think of that night. She was eight years old, and he walked through the door breaking the man's arm in several places. He had scooped Liz up and demanded that the woman get Liz's belongings. He carried her out of the house, took her to a safe place and tended to her many injuries.

"They thought they could beat the witch out of me."

Lucas roared with laughter. He walked over and kissed her.

"It's amazing how your humor works."

"That's me... Carrot Top the Comedian. Now, may I go feed my chickens?"

He gave a slight nod. He took in the first page of notes before he made his way downstairs. He walked out with her. It was cold and gray. He now understood her attire, as hideous as it was, he understood. She had grabbed a thick fur lined coat before she walked out.

Liz learned how to hunt from her last foster parents. They had been good people and treated Liz with respect and kindness. Liz respected the land and only hunted for what she needed to survive. She wasted nothing on the animal. Her real parents had shown her how to determine what foods were edible in the wild such as berries, nuts, and mushrooms. Her father had shown her how to tan hides. She remembered that when she had killed her first deer, and her foster dad was showing her the technique of tanning the hide. The memories of her biological parents were there, but they were few and far between.

Lucas walked several paces behind her so he could take in the land and their surroundings. The air felt heavy and oppressive. It was November, but it felt wrong. Liz spun around and looked past Lucas. She placed her fingers to her lips and whistled. Two dogs busted out from a pen that was fifty feet from behind the house. They ran past Lucas straight to Liz. They were two very sleek beautiful Dobermans. Liz leaned down and spoke in Russian; the dogs began growling and snarling.

"Lucas please join me. Slow and easy." Liz's voice had a hitch to it.

A warning with a touch of fear. He slowly walked up to her. She reached her hand out and he took it. She spoke again in whispered Russian. The dogs walked over to Lucas and smelled him.

"Now, they know you."

A command was given, and the dogs took off. There was a lot of growling then yelping from the barn area. One of the dogs came back with a limp form in her mouth. The other dog walked back beside the other. Liz stroked both dogs.

"Good Prissy, please drop it. Sassy, good girl. Both, sit."

Prissy dropped the limp form in front of Liz. Sassy took two steps back and sat down. Prissy stayed beside Sassy. Lucas bent down.

"Liz, get in the house, now. Take them with you. No one gets in the house except me." Liz didn't move.

"Liz, please."

She shook her head.

"This is a hellhound."

"I know what it is and I'm not leaving you to deal with them."

Lucas bit his lip so he wouldn't cuss, throw her over his shoulder, and carry her back to the house. She touched his back.

"Can we just do this together? I have a plan." She told him.

He looked at her. Another command was given to the dogs. Prissy stood and picked up the limp form in front of Liz. She turned and pranced to the front porch. Sassy stood and fell in step beside Prissy. Liz walked to the back door. Lucas was not happy. He followed. He did not speak until they were in the house. Liz looked at him.

"Lucas, you knew they would come sooner or later."

"I was hoping for later. They will not touch you this time."

She smiled a radiant smile.

"I know," she said.

She closed the door behind them and bolted it. She held the doorknob and closed her eyes for a minute. He felt it, he felt her magic.

"I refuse to live always looking over my shoulder as my mother did. I refuse to be alone because of fear of my neighbor. Most of all, I refuse to let my children hear my dying ear-piercing screams."

She walked past Lucas to the front door and ordered Prissy and Sassy in. The hellhound was left so his owners could see that she was not running. Liz closed the door once the dogs were in, held the knob as she did the back door, then she turned and walked up the stairs. Prissy laid on the mat just inside the door. Sassy went to the back door and laid at the mat in front of that door. Commands were given in Russian, both dogs were on full alert. Lucas followed her up the stairs. Once they were in the attic, Lucas walked up behind her, leaned his head down to her shoulder, turned his head to face her neck, breathed in her scent, and kissed her neck.

"Liz, will you ever allow me to do my job as your protector?"

"You have time and time again. Now it is my turn to protect myself, my home, and my love." She reached her hand up to his face and stroked his cheek.

Lucas was blown away. "What?"

"Can you live without me?"

"No."

"And I can't live without you."

Lucas took her hand. "Liz, what are you saying?"

"If you want to leave you can, but if you want to stay, then I am asking you to stay with me in my home as my protector and my partner."

"Do you know what you are asking?"

"I do. Now I have work to do."

Lucas took her shoulders and turned her to face him. "I am your protector, and I will not leave you."

He ripped her shirt open, and the buttons went flying everywhere. The chill of the room touched her skin. She grabbed the front of his shirt and pulled him close.

"Lucas, are you sure?"

He didn't answer her with words. He showed her how absolute his answer was, he wasn't leaving. He would protect her and love her until the end of their days. He was humbled by the fact that she would make her request known.

The Call

The day began to pass quickly, night was approaching. Prissy howled and started growling. Liz was in Lucas' shirt and her jeans. She stood, lit six white candles and one black candle, she sat cross legged on the floor and mentally began working through her spell. Lucas ran downstairs and grabbed his staff from his duster then he ran back to Liz.

"They are near."

"I know."

Lucas spun his staff and pounded the floor with it three times. Liz's spell came to life.

"I call thee enemy of my blood."

Lucas spun around. "What the hell are you doing Liz?" He growled his frustration.

"I told you I have a plan."

"Damn it!"

She smiled, "trust me, please."

Ten agonizing minutes later there was a crash at the front door. Lucas took a deep breath he sensed seven people. Liz walked over to her largest Atlas and quickly read her notes.

"Seven won't do, their numbers shall drop to five."

She reached behind a box, pulled out a pair of silver knives with ivory handles. She pushed on the small round window and threw the blade with a twist of her wrist. No magic was used so the Blackthornes didn't sense anything out of the ordinary, that was until the knife sliced through the youngest man's neck. When his brother turned to help him, he was hit with a second blade. None of the men present ever saw the window open. It was closed as soon as the blades left her hands. It was sealed with a spell as soon as it was closed. All of the windows and doors were sealed and would only open at her command or Lucas' command.

The Blackthornes were furious. They had the numbers and no Krimshaw would leave this place alive. Mark reached in his pocket, pulled out his phone and called his grandmother.

"Two are dead." He responded to the question on the other end of the phone. "Luke and Seth."

He quickly pulled the phone away from his ear. The others present could hear the yelling from where they stood. They were ordered to wait until Katherine Blackthorne arrived. She would be there before midnight. It was only nine at night, so they had plenty of time to wait, guards were posted around the house. Mark shivered from the cold and thought of someone upsetting his grandmother, Katherine. You would have to be a fool to do that. Liz and Lucas continued working inside the house. Liz's plan was falling into place. She would make Katherine hear her family's screams and watch their demise before Katherine finally fell onto Liz's blade. Katherine was the reason for Liz's family's sufferings; Liz had had enough. Lucas could feel Liz's anger. He tried to send calming thoughts and vibes to her.

"DON'T."

Lucas jumped from the authority in her tone. "Liz, please."

She walked over to him and gently placed her hand at his temple. He was blasted with images of the past. He had heard those facts from his father's father.

"How did you know all of that?"

"Why do you think I love working in the archive department? Research of course."

He just looked at her. There was information there that was not in the archive department, it was too detailed and gruesome. She knew how to mask her magic, which was an exceedingly difficult task even for a seasoned witch, but she had mastered it. Even he could not sense all of her magic and he was in the room with her. He stood tall and lightly tapped his staff. Liz walked to the far wall to retrieve a black leather backpack. She opened the backpack to double-check its contents. Lucas was working on protective shields around them and the property. He watched as she took each item out. The bag contained daggers, dried dehydrated fruits, dried dehydrated veggies, a thick leather-bound book with Krimshaw on the front, a shoe box labeled Special Gifts (ages 6-34years), a poncho, and extra socks. She repacked everything with perfection.

Realization struck him. "Liz the box labeled Special Gifts..."

"Yes."

"Are those the items I gave you?"

"Of course. Who else would they be from?"

"You know when this is over we are going to work on your sarcasm."

"Nope," she shook her head and smiled.

She pulled out a second backpack to check its contents. He quickly realized she had packed him a ruck sack as well. He just stared at her. She always seemed to be one step ahead of him and better prepared than MacGyver ever could be. She pulled a small box out from where she had the backpacks hid. She pulled out thermals, stripped, put on the thermals, and redressed. She threw Lucas a shirt.

"Its cold out, I'd hate for you to freeze because you're dressed like that." She winked at him.

"Keep on and you will be dressed in far less than I am."

"Oh, such promises. You can spoil me later."

He took a step toward her. "How about now and later?"

He took another step and smacked into an invisible wall. She started laughing. He tapped the shield with his staff and walked through her shield. She started laughing but was stopped with kisses. She caught her breath long enough to tell him that it had to wait because Katherine was on the move. He made promises for later and got into position. Liz picked up the shirt off the floor and handed it to him. It was a warm black flannel shirt. She also handed him warm black wool socks.

"If we have to leave, we will go to our first hideout. It is ready and waiting. Oh, when this is over, I am taking my last name back."

"You don't like my forefather's sir name?"

"Yes, however I am tired of hiding."

"What about my last name?"

"It has not been offered."

He gently touched her face and kissed her. They had work to do, they both knew it. The time ticked by, but neither moved. The dogs began to growl. Liz looked at her watch, 11:35p.m. She whistled and the dogs ran up the stairs to join her.

"Ladies no intruders get by you!"

She repeated the command in Russian and stepped forward. Lucas stepped beside her and the dogs flanked left and right of them. Liz closed her eyes and began swaying, the room cracked with energy, but it was not just hers. Lucas was a protector for a reason. You would not want to ever cross him on a bad day. Liz's necklace tingled against her skin. She smiled.

"Always on the job."

"Yes ma'am."

"We will see if I can remove work from your mind later."

He smiled and had brief images flash in his mind of just how she would distract him later. If he had only known her desires years ago. He shook his head to clear the thoughts of what could have been. The time was now, and she had expressed her desires. It was time to work. He stood straight, looked at Liz, and took her hand. They were together and they would defeat the Blackthornes, one way or another. He spun his staff, and the energy popped around them. Liz smiled at him.

"About time."

"Liz!"

"Lucas." She batted her lashes at him. He felt a slight zing go up his arm. He didn't jump, it didn't hurt, but he knew she was giving her own warning.

Righting the Wrongs of the Past

Katherine arrived. She may be in her mid-eighties, but she didn't look a day over fifty. That would soon change. The second her foot touched Liz's property line, the air crackled with magical energy.

"You fool, it was a trap."

Mark was running to his grandmother's aide when an arrow pierced his shoulder. He screamed in agony. Katherine was mouthing counter spells, but nothing was allowing her or her family to leave the property. Katherine had people running perimeter checks for two weeks. No sign of magic was ever detected. Katherine had even had distant relatives going into ask for archives, no one picked up on anything. It was believed that she was not a practicing Krimshaw, which should have made this easy. She always believed that Liz had a protector like Liz's grandmother once had. In fact, she was sure of it on the night of Liz's fifteenth birthday. Katherine made sure that Liz would feel pain before she was to be killed that night. To her horror, Liz had survived, and it was Katherine's son, her precious son, Juan, who had paid the price. He returned with his hands amputated and a description of a man who ended Liz's torture. Juan died shortly after he gave the description.

Katherine had tracked and searched for years. One day she passed Liz inside the bank and her skin tingled. Her warning of a Krimshaw being nearby. Liz had not let on that she felt anything. A year later she hears that her niece's son is planning to go out with a woman named Liz and how much he liked her. Once her sister gave her the description that her niece had given her, Katherine put a stop to it. That was almost a year ago. Katherine had followed her several times after that, she started making plans to get rid of the final two Krimshaw children.

She had heard there was another child from neighbors of Liz's parents, though no one knew if it was a boy or a girl. That told Katherine that the baby was born at home or away, but not at the hospital. Mark had been soft on finding the boy and making his adopted mother talk. That was why Katherine had intervened as a reminder and warning not to mess with the Blackthornes. Katherine was mentally reflecting on the last thirty years when there was an ear-piercing noise, but no one knew where it was coming from. Levi grabbed his head and screamed. His ears were bleeding and so were his eyes. His last breath was pure agony. Katherine became very angry.

"Enough!" Katherine bellowed.

Nothing happened. She walked toward the house and an arrow grazed her ear.

"I will kill you for that."

The noise grew louder and shriller. Liz, Lucas, and the dogs couldn't hear it. Liz took every precaution she could when she set her traps. Liz sat on the floor and began chanting while Lucas circled her three times, stopping at the exact location he began. Liz lifted a wooden lid off a box that was on the floor beside the table. She pulled out a small piece of rope, salt, and an old hat. He knew the hat. Why did he know the hat? He quickly thought about the images from earlier. He gasped; it was Katherine's hat from when all of this began. How did Liz get that hat? His eyes grew wide. She was reversing magic and time with that hat. She was in deep concentration; she tied the hat and sprinkled it with salt.

"Age defied time and time again. Original owner of this hat age defied no more. For every minute you shall age a year until you have reached your actual age. Looks are not all that goes, oh no...so shall your health."

She was creating a spell. His grandfather spoke of such things from her grandmother. Yes of course, it skipped generations, plus it fell to twins. Spinners were rare and only a couple still existed.

"Your grandmother was a twin, but you're not."

"I was, but my twin died in embryo. My grandmother's mom was born with a veil over her face."

"The mark of a powerful visionary or a seer."

"We call it the witch's veil or third eye."

"You amaze me."

"Just wait, it gets better."

The dogs' fur were standing on end, and they were growling. Several loud thuds were hitting the front door. Nothing and no one were getting in, not yet anyway. Mark had finally got the arrow out with the assistance of Ashton. They quickly realized that was a mistake because Ashton's hands were blistering and Mark's whole shoulder was swollen and festering. Liz took a glass of water and poured a few drops on the mirror that lay on the floor in front of her. She was scrying. She could see exactly what was happening. Katherine walked over and said a healing spell. Mark dropped to his knees.

"Stop. Stop. It burns horribly."

Katherine realized her spells were having the opposite effect, so she decided to say it backwards. Liz had planned for this too, Mark fell over and began writhing, screaming, and swearing. The convulsions were violent. Katherine stood.

"Get that door open or burn the house down. I don't care which occurs just make it happen. The young witch is mine."

Katherine held Mark until he passed. Xavier and Alec gathered straw from the barn and placed it around the house. Alec pulled out a lighter and lit the straw. Xavier was too close, Liz opened the small window, said a silent spell, and watched as the flame ignited and caught Xavier's clothing on fire. Alec grabbed Xavier and threw him to the ground. Lucas could smell smoke.

"Liz be ready."

She shook her head. "Not yet."

She said another silent spell and the flames were extinguished.

Lucas kissed her. "I guess I can sit this one out since you have this under control."

She laughed, "it's your hide not mine."

"Liz, she's coming."

She winked. "I know, now be ready because she comes with a new vengeance."

"New...oh boy!" Sarcasm rolled off his tongue.

Prissy and Sassy gave a low whine. Liz stood and took her place. Lucas took his place in front of her, turned, kissed her, and turned back around. The front door crashed open. Katherine started to walk when she saw her hand. Alec gapped at his great grandmother. Katherine's joints wore stiff. It hurt to walk.

"You look so old!" Alec said.

"Alec enough!"

Liz waited until both were in the house before she threw her next spell. Alec helped his great grandmother up the steps. Every time he looked at her, she looked older. He was extremely concerned. They entered the house with caution. Katherine performed several old tracing spells, nothing was revealed. She walked into the living room; she saw the piano and spun to face her great grandson.

"Get out!"

Alec stepped toward her, she shook her head, he turned for the door and it slammed shut. He pulled on the doorknob, and it was hot.

Fear didn't even describe what he was feeling. He didn't sign up for this, he was with his father when the call came in.

"Great grandmother, what did she ever do to you?"

"How dare you question me." She mumbled something and he fell to his knees.

"I have every right to question you. You are risking my dad's life and mine. I have a right to know why."

Liz stepped around Lucas; the dogs followed. Lucas swore. Liz walked down the stairs with her back perfectly straight.

"I agree Katherine. He has a right to know why he will die tonight because of you."

"You retched crow, I will kill you."

Liz's spell hit Katherine hard and knocked her across the room. "I think not!"

Lucas stepped by Liz and placed his arm around her waist with his hand on her hip. His staff in his other hand. "I agree. You will never touch her again," Lucas said.

"Again?" Alec asked.

Liz turned around and raised her shirts so Alec could see her back. The scars were clear. Alec gagged. When he could finally speak, he was very pale.

"How was that done and by who?"

"Her dear son Juan, which is why he lost his hands to my blade," Lucas said with little restraint.

"A dull blade heated and a cattle brand," Liz said. She was addressing Alec's question.

Alec was horrified at the thought. He turned to face his great grandmother. "Did you order that?"

"I ordered worse."

"You are foul. I can't believe you would hurt someone like that," Alec shuddered as he said it.

"She has done much worse over the years; would you like to tell him, or would you like me to?"

Katherine threw a spell cutting Lucas' cheek. Liz's fury was no match for this horrible woman because Katherine went flying across the room. Alec embraced his heritage, but he unleashed on his great grandmother not on Liz. Katherine's death would not be on Liz's conscience if he could help it. Liz and Lucas stepped forward and stopped Alec.

"No, you will never forgive yourself and then this feud will continue," Liz said as she touched Alec's hand. She gently lowered his hand and met his eyes.

Liz had not intended for any of the Blackthornes to leave alive, but she was making one exception. If she made it a blanket execution, she would be no better than the one who started this feud and that was the woman crumpled on the floor.

"Please sit, I want you to know her sins, so you can ensure it no longer continues."

Alec was humming with energy, he couldn't stand the sight of his great grandmother since he realized her intentions, and seeing Liz's back made him physically ill. The word monster didn't even come close to describing Katherine Blackthorne in his mind, Alec stood like he'd been shot. Lucas went on high alert. Alec was shaking with fury.

"My mom didn't kill herself, did she?"

Lucas looked at Liz with a look of confusion and she shrugged.

"Sure, she did." Katherine laughed and blood came from her mouth and nose. "She accidentally pulled the little space heater into the tub."

"Accidentally isn't suicide," he vibrated with energy as he spoke.

"Tell me you HAG!"

"She was a meddling fool."

Lucas and Liz stepped back. The front door flew open. Sassy and Prissy growled. Xavier was burned badly, and Ashton was covered in blisters.

"Don't!" Alec bellowed to the others. He would not let them advance any further. "She killed my mother," Alec was pointing at Katherine. Alec's voice was laced with fury as he addressed the two men of his family. "Liz is going to speak and you two will listen."

"Like hell," growled Ashton.

"Then get out," Alec said.

He spun, said a spell knocking the two men out the door and the door slammed shut. Alec didn't think he simply spun around and sent his great grandmother into the air. He chanted and sang when she fell to the ground, she was very broken and barely breathing. Alec walked over so she could see his face.

"Your death is on you." Alec spoke the killing spell and walked back to the couch and looked at Liz and Lucas. "My mother meant the world to me. I always thought there was more to her death."

Lucas said a silent spell of protection for Liz, touched her shoulder, and walked to the door. He had to deal with Ashton and Xavier before they tried to burn the house down again.

Alec looked at Liz, "please tell me."

Where It All Began

Liz walked to the kitchen, assured Alec she'd be right back, got herself a large glass of wine, and Alec a glass of water. She walked back into the living room with the weight of the world on her shoulders. She sat down, sipped her wine, and began the tale.

> "The year was 1946, my grandmother was a sophomore, and Katherine was a senior in high school. They were friends, they knew what they were and embraced it. My grandmother had a natural talent in both sports and music. She caught the attention of Sherwan Krimshaw. Sherwan's best friend, Michael Blackthorne, was kind of shy, but really liked Katherine. Sherwan asked Lucy, my grandmother, out and asked if it could be a double date. Katherine agreed to the date, but she secretly had her eye on Sherwan not Michael.
>
> It was obvious that Sherwan only had eyes for Lucy. After the double date Sherwan and Lucy were inseparable as were Katherine and Michael. That June Sherwan, Michael, and Katherine graduated. Lucy would be a junior and her parents wouldn't let

her quit school to get married, so Sherwan became the blacksmith's apprentice. He saved as much as he could to buy land to prove to Lucy's parents that he would and could provide for her. He built a two-room cabin on the land. Michael went to law school and Katherine became his wife, though she never loved him.

Lucy would go over to Katherine's house at least once a week. She had no idea that Katherine desired Sherwan. Lucy's senior year, her parents agreed to allow her to marry with the understanding that she had to finish school. Two months after they were wed, she became pregnant. Thankfully, graduation was only two months away so she wouldn't be showing. Lucy and Katherine saw each other daily after Lucy graduated.

When Lucy revealed she was pregnant to Katherine, Katherine lost it. She started ranting about how unfair it was and how she should be with Sherwan not Michael. Lucy stood telling Katherine to grow up and left. Lucy told Sherwan about what happened, and he became furious. They went back to see Michael and Katherine. Sherwan told Michael everything, but Katherine had another tale to tale. She said that Sherwan tried to seduce her two weeks prior. Michael believed his wife over his best friend and there began the betrayals. Katherine became pregnant not long after that. Michael didn't realize it wasn't his child until three years later when he caught his wife with one of the hired hands. He beat them both relentlessly. He asked her two questions afterwards; Did Sherwan really try to seduce you? And is Juan

MIDNIGHT THE WITCHING HOUR

mine?

She answered no to both. He locked her in a room for a year. She was only allowed out to eat and go to the bathroom. He made sure her next child was his. Michael called on Sherwan and Lucy a day after he caught Katherine in the affair. He apologized to them for his ignorance. When Lucy asked where Katherine was at, he allowed her to see her. Lucy couldn't believe her eyes. Katherine was black and blue, and her face was swollen. Lucy demanded herbs and clean water so she could help Katherine heal. She worked on her healing for hours. When she was done Katherine spoke.

"Lucy McKay Krimshaw, I blame you for this and I will make you and your family pay generation after generation, now begone with you."

Lucy stood and spoke to her former friend. "You ungrateful woman. You were the one sleeping with another man and desiring another woman's husband. You only have yourself to blame."

Lucy knocked three times and was allowed out of the room. She walked down the hall with her back straight and head high, not once looking back at the room. A year passed and Katherine gave birth to twin boys, she despised them. Their nanny raised them because Katherine wanted nothing to do with them. Michael knew she was a witch and forbid her from practicing. The hired help that she had the affair with was beaten and thrown into the dungeons. He got a horrible infection and died a week later. Katherine grieved horribly. Michael allowed Katherine out of the room after the birth of the twins. She returned to their room with anger in her heart.

Several months passed before she sought her revenge on Michael. She had noticed one of the teenage servants eyeing Michael, so Katherine made arrangements for the young servant to meet her in her bed chambers late one night. When Michael arrived, he was surprised to see Katherine brushing the teenager's hair. The girl was in one of Katherine's nightgowns.

"What's this?"

"A gift for my discretions. Take her and have her satisfy you in a wifely way. You deserve someone young and fresh."

The girl stood and bowed. "I'm sorry Ma'am that was not why I came here."

"Oh, but it is."

Katherine stood, walked out, and locked the door. Michael was not gentle with the young servant. Her screams could be heard throughout the home. The next morning, she could barely walk. Michael visited her every night for two weeks until she finally hung herself. Every female servant feared Michael, but they feared his cruel wife even more. They were never caught looking at Michael. One night Katherine was performing her wifely duties, pulled a blade from under the mattress and slit his throat just as he was relieving himself inside her. That was the night that she became pregnant with Michael's daughter.

She made three female servants remove the body, change the sheets, and clean the room. Katherine told everyone that Michael went to New York on business. His body was found two weeks later with his throat slit and his body beaten. Everyone thought he was mugged. The three female servants were sold to the local brothel. All were virgins when they left her home. The day her daughter was born was the day she made plans to go after Lucy. She had to plan everything with precision. She had nothing but time.

Years had passed since Lucy had gone to Katherine's aide, however Lucy and Sherwan knew better than to let their guards down. Lucy was out hanging up clothes when four men slipped up behind her and kidnapped her, Lucy's oldest son recognized one of the men and grabbed up all of his siblings and ran to his father's blacksmith shop. Lucy was brought to Katherine's home and locked in the room where Katherine had once been held prisoner. Lucy fought with every ounce of her being. She fought physically and magically. Katherine overpowered her because Lucy was pregnant with her seventh child. Katherine cut out her tongue and sent it to Sherwan, then she cut the child out of Lucy's stomach. She took the child from the room and left my grandmother to die. She nursed the baby girl as if she were her own, but after a week the baby died. Sherwan came that night with two lawmen at his side. Katherine lied about seeing Lucy. Her body was dumped three days later on Sherwan's doorstep. Katherine packed up her home and the servants the night the law came. When they returned, the day Lucy's body arrived, the house was completely empty."

Liz's glass was empty. Lucas walked back into the house, went to their room, and changed clothes. Liz had clothes in her closet for him. She excused herself and went to go get more wine. When she returned Alec was white as a ghost.

"Why did Michael hurt the girl?"

"He was full of hatred caused by his wife."

"She was a horrible, horrible person."

"You sure you want to hear the rest?"

"Yes."

Lucas walked out and kissed Liz. She had allowed him to do his job, now all he wanted was to make her happy. Liz sipped her wine, then picked up where she left off.

"My father was Sherwan and Lucy's oldest son and a powerful mage. He was skilled at farming, even at a young age he had a green thumb. At seventeen his youngest brother was involved in a hunting accident. Sherwan explained to all of their children Katherine's words and the threat of the curse that was relayed to Lucy on that day in the locked room. When the accident occurred to the youngest child, none of the Krimshaws believed it was an accident. Sherwan made sure all of his sons were trained properly in fighting, trade, and magic. One by one Sherwan's sons were picked off, over the years.

Katherine made it clear that Sherwan was to be left untouched. He died a few months after my parents were killed. Even though Katherine did not come after my grandfather, in the end it was due to her that he died. He died of a broken heart. He lost his wife and their children because of jealousy. Katherine could say that she loved my grandfather, but she never loved anyone except herself, and she loved power.

The last one remaining was my dad. When he met my mom, four of his siblings were still alive. He kept nothing from my mother. She immediately began looking over her shoulder for fear that they were next. They didn't have me until my mother was thirty-six, because of the fear. Her pregnancy with my brother was unnerving for us all. When I was five, two days after my brother was born, that fear became a reality. Two men broke down our front door with magic, I grabbed my brother and went to the cellar, I could hear the thudding of boots walking so I knew there were more than two men. I sat in that cellar hearing blows being landed to my parents, and ear-piercing screams from my mother. As soon as I grabbed my brother, I placed a calming charm on him so he wouldn't cry and a silencing charm so he wouldn't hear all the bad. I couldn't risk performing that charm for myself because I had to know what was happening and where everyone was at within the house."

Lucas wrapped his arms around Liz in a comforting and protective manner. He hated that she had to relive these nightmares. He knew she re-lived those memories every night in her sleep, but to tell them to a stranger was too much for anyone. She patted his hand, as a reassurance that she was fine.

"The beatings and screams continued for hours, then I smelt smoke. My home was on fire and my fear was for my brother's safety. That was when Lucas arrived. He saved us. The next day my brother and I began two different lives. I went from foster home to foster home. Twice, the Blackthornes found me, the first time I escaped before my foster parents suffered. The second time I wasn't so lucky. Juan busted in my home when I was fifteen, it was at midnight. My foster parents didn't know of my abilities, but Juan tortured them with magic, left them to die, and set their home ablaze, but before that occurred, he made them watch me being tortured. She pointed to her back. He tortured me, then them, he drug me out the door on my bloody back by my ankle and lit the house as he was walking out. I could hear their screams. He drug me to the barn and grabbed the branding iron to continue his work. Lucas arrived and stopped the torture.

Lucas was bloody and beaten when he arrived. He had sensed the Blackthornes a week prior to Juan arriving. He tracked them to a farmhouse twenty miles away, there were ten of them and only one of him. He sensed one was solo, but he had to deal with the ten before he could go after the one. Once I was in his care, he carried me to the river and collapsed. His injuries were bad. I knew of an old farmhouse down the road from where I lived. I did what I could at the river to keep him alive as well as myself. The water burned my tortured skin, and I knew it had to do the same to his skin, but I had to get him clean. The hours ticked by. I feared Juan or another Blackthorne would return. Finally, Lucas came around. He was furious with himself for collapsing, but he didn't realize how bad his wounds were. He carried me to a safe place, tended to my wounds, and a week later he brought me here. I have been here for twenty years.

This land is the original Krimshaw land. The little building I use for my art studio is part of the original cabin. My name was changed when I was five to Liz Briley, which was the reason Katherine hadn't come sooner because there was no family history to Briley on my mother's side or my grandmother's side. Katherine thought a Krimshaw would never be foolish enough to return here. This land was loved and cherished by Sherwan and Lucy. They are buried here along with five of their sons. My father and mother's ashes were sprinkled over the river the day we set out on my new life. The location of the daughter's remains was only known by Katherine.

This land has power for the Krimshaw family but no one else. I immediately felt the power the day we arrived. Lucas felt it too, though he just thought it was history. Before Katherine had her grandsons and her great-grandsons invade my home, she sent others to pay my brother and his adopted seventy-two-year-old mother a visit. Mark went easy on my brother, but Katherine returned and tortured Morning Star when she didn't talk, she tortured her more in front of the locals as a warning.

Alec stood abruptly, "bathroom?"

He was so pale. Lucas quickly showed him to the bathroom and stood outside the door to make sure he didn't go anywhere else in the house.

Forgiveness

Alec returned to the living room. "Sorry it's hard to stomach."

"Understandable," Liz said.

Lucas went to the kitchen to make tea.

"Coffee please."

"If you insist." Coffee was her beverage of choice not his. Lucas smiled.

Liz looked at Alec. "I nor Lucas have ever given leniency before, so why should it be given to you?"

"She repulses me. No one should've had to go through what you've been through. I will correct the Blackthorne history."

"Touch my hand and tell me what you feel." Liz said.

Alec touched her hand, he wasn't sure what he was supposed to feel, because he wasn't feeling anything except the warmth of her skin. He shook his head. "I feel the warmth of your skin. That's it."

Lucas walked behind Alec. He could sense if he was lying or not. He was telling the truth; he gave a silent nod to Liz. Lucas walked to the fireplace and built a fire. The house had a noticeable chill.

"Will you please take out the trash?"

"Yes, after the fire is going good."

"Thank you."

"Sir, what happened to your face? Were the Blackthornes behind it?" Alec asked. He wasn't rude or hateful. He was curious and sincere.

Liz was the one who took on the protector roll this time. She stood and quickly went to his side at the fireplace. Lucas roared with laughter. He wrapped his arm around her and kissed the top of her head.

"Liz, it has been twenty years I am well past it." Lucas took her hand and looked at Alec. "Yes, it was from the Blackthornes. The night Juan tortured Liz and we went to the old farmhouse, Katherine paid revenge for her son's hands. She sent her daughter, Zandria, to finish what Juan started. We were asleep. I believe a sleeping charm and a silencing charm were cast because neither of us felt her nor heard her. Zandria's nickname was Zay like slay, but with a z. She was ruthless."

Liz kissed Lucas' cheek. "Not near as ruthless as you."

Alec turned his head away and blushed when Liz kissed Lucas. Lucas cleared his throat.

"Anyway, I awoke to the smell of smoke. I jumped up but was disoriented. Liz ran to my side, but I told her to get out and I would follow. I couldn't get a grip on where I was or what was happening, the next thing I knew I was outside, and Liz was splashing me with water."

"You're not burned," Alec stated.

Liz raised her right sleeve so he could see the scarred flesh. He cringed.

"What about Zandria?"

"I tracked her down."

"And?"

"Buried her."

Alec stared at Lucas.

"You might as well drop it, because that will be the best explanation you will get," Liz said.

Alec looked at his great grandmother's dead body, then back to Liz and Lucas. "We were all pawns in her game. We were all expendable including her favorite child, Juan."

He sat down on the floor and placed his hands in his face. Lucas took Liz's hand.

"How old are you, Alec?"

"Sixteen."

"Where will you go?"

"My aunt's house. She is my mom's sister."

Lucas walked over to Alec and placed his hands on the side of Alec's head. He took a deep breath. Alec spoke the truth, and he didn't have anyone else. He also couldn't believe all of this was based on his great grandmother's jealousy. So many, too many, people lost their lives for nothing. Liz's family didn't deserve this. Lucas opened his eyes and nodded to Liz.

"Do you promise to right the history?" Liz asked.

"Yes, if you have copies of any documents, my aunt will help me. She works for a big publishing company in Colorado. She despised my great grandmother. She tried to get my mother too leave before her death. My aunt will be thrilled to sink the Blackthornes."

"Call her. You will stay here until she can get you a flight out or she gets here."

"She'll have a flight booked as soon as I call."

"You can't go back to get clothes or anything."

"I have everything I need." Alec pulled a thick necklace out of the collar of his sweatshirt.

"It was my mother's." He looked at Lucas.

"If we go to my great grandmother's SUV, I will give you access to her accounts."

"We aren't thieves." Liz hissed at Alec.

He shook his head. "I never said that."

Lucas calmed Liz before she changed her mind about forgiveness. He looked at Alec and motioned him to the kitchen. Alec was quick. Prissy and Sassy were laying on a mat near the fire. The quick movement set them on full alert. They stood and started growling. Liz walked over to stand between them. She stroked their heads, but she did not issue a command. Lucas smiled and tapped his staff. The dogs laid back down. Liz started laughing. Lucas made Alec sit down at the kitchen table.

"Liz has everything she needs. She believes in working for what she has, not handouts. The money is yours and your aunts. Now call her."

Lucas stepped out of the kitchen and returned to the living room. He kissed Liz on the cheek then picked up Katherine's body and started to walk out.

"Not on the land."

"I know not to taint it."

She laughed. Lucas returned to the house about twenty minutes later. Alec was still on the phone with his aunt. She made him stay on the phone while she went online to book his flight. Liz slipped in and handed him some paper. He looked at her strangely.

"To write down the information."

"She'll send everything to my phone."

Liz turned, swore, and walked back to her room. She gathered all the extra copies of the supporting documents and placed them in a leather briefcase. She had an extra flash drive as well and stuck it in an envelope. She was no fool, the originals were placed safely away from her home, that way she or Lucas could retrieve them if forced to flee. She had also taken precautions in the event they were killed and how the info would reach the appropriate sources. She would give Alec and his aunt a year at most to make amends for his retched family ties, then she would take matters into her own hands.

Alec's flight was scheduled for three hours from now. That would give them time to get Alec to the airport and check in. Lucas drove Alec to the ATM so he could make a considerable withdrawal. Liz stayed at home waiting for Lucas' return. He did a sweep of the area before he left to make sure there were no remaining threats. He drove Liz's old Ford truck to the airport. Alec was silent the whole way to the airport. Lucas knew he was trying to make sense of everything.

"There is nothing to sort out."

"I don't get it."

"That's good. Jealousy is hard to understand."

"Why hold onto it for so long?"

Lucas only shrugged. He didn't have the answers because he didn't understand it himself. Lucas knew that Liz had a back-up plan if Alec's aunt couldn't get this to print. He didn't know what the plan or plans were, however, he knew Liz and without a doubt he knew she had at least one or two back-up plans.

Once at the airport Alec checked in. The bag with all the historical information was a carry-on. Lucas stayed, explained the timeline, gave him Liz's mailing address and phone number, then watched Alec board the plane. He waited until the plane was in the air and a distant spot on the horizon before he left. When Lucas walked into Liz's house, he smelled white sage and lilacs, there was slow rhythmic jazz playing and candles burning in the living room. Liz welcomed him home as if he had been away for years. Peace filled the room as they made love time and time again.

Results

A year had passed, and Alec had kept his word. His aunt was thrilled to take on this project. She may work for a publisher, but she is also a New York Times bestselling author in nonfiction and children's literature. When she saw all the data against Katherine Blackthorne, the writer in her took control. She had a ninety-thousand-word manuscript written in two months, she edited it to the best of her ability, then pitched it to her current agent.

The agent loved it and sent it to several publishers, there were several interested, and one accepted it immediately with high royalty pay out, international rights, and before it was said and done there were also movie and tv rights offered. Joanna took out any reference for magic so it would be presented as historical fiction. She had met Katherine when her sister married Mark. Mark seemed ok besides the fact that he was always doing whatever Katherine said. Katherine did hold the purse strings for the whole Blackthorne family, but there always seemed to be something more to it than that. Now she knew.

Joanna would avenge her sister's murder and lay out all of Katherine's deep dark secrets. She had all the documentation needed if anyone ever questioned her for proof. She too was no fool; she made three copies of everything. One copy was sent to an undisclosed location, one copy went to her publisher, and the other copy was placed in a safety deposit box that required two keys and a password. The copy in her possession was believed by most to be the only copy. Her publisher had met her privately and asked for a copy. He expressed his concerns for retaliation or vengeance from the Blackthorne family. He wanted them covered.

Joanna had never trusted people at face value, so she had agreed, but told him it would take time to copy and burn another flash drive. She made him wait two weeks before she gave him his copy. Of course, the copies were made long before the publisher had accepted it. She made him wait so she could investigate to see if there were any Blackthorne ties; family or business once that was ruled out, she released his copy to him and swore him to secrecy. This was the best book he had ever represented, there was no way he would mess it up by destroying client confidence. Alec was home with Joanna when the delivery truck arrived. There were five hundred books for Joanna's upcoming book signing. She opened the first box and took out three books, one for herself, Alec, and the woman who made it possible, Liz.

Tuesday October 31st Liz opened her mailbox to find a brown paper wrapped package. She gently ran her hand over the return label. She slowly walked back to the house. Lucas had been watching from the window. He went to the door to greet her. Joanna had shared the rough draft with Liz before she ever sent it to her agent, she then sent another copy once the publishing house editor had gotten a hold of it, but this was different. This was the final copy. The one that the world would see. Joy and a sense of closure filled Liz. She walked into the house and Lucas greeted her with a kiss.

She touched her swollen stomach. "No more fear or running little one."

Lucas took the package from Liz, took her left hand, and led her to the couch. He sat beside her and together they opened the package. The cover was blue green with a red rose being held by a dark shadow figure of a woman. The thorns of the rose were dripping with blood. The title was in white calligraphy letters. *Jealousy, Lies, and Destruction. A True Reflection of the Many Lives Destroyed by a Woman's Treachery; The Chronicles of Katherine Blackthorne!*

Inside the front cover was a note. Dearest Liz, thank you so much for saving my nephew, finding out the truth about my sister's death, and allowing me to bring closure to your family's nightmare. If you would like to come to New York sometime there are two tickets in the back of the book. Thank you doesn't even begin to tell you, the magnitude of my gratitude. I hope one day we can sit, talk, and have a cup of coffee.

Lucas kissed her neck. "Well... the wicked witch is dead."

Liz started laughing. "Where is the bucket of water and her broom?"

"Well, her SUV is crushed in the junk yard and her body will remain in an undisclosed location."

''Thank you." She turned and wrapped her arms around him.

"I will always protect you."

"A witch and a protector mated. Our child will be beyond powerful."

He touched her stomach. He grinned. "A Realm Walker or Portal Keeper."

"What?"

"A shifter between worlds. One who can become anyone. That or a medicine..."

He started to speak the gender of the baby when Liz placed her finger to his lips. She didn't want to know the gender until the child was born. Lucas wanted to tell her desperately.

"Three more months love."

"A lifetime from now."

The year since Katherine's passing had been good for them. Lucas' family had stopped by several months ago. All the men in his family were powerful protectors and they absolutely adored Liz.

Any woman who could love and be loved by the seventh son of a seventh son was perfect in their book. If their child was a boy, he too would be a protector. If they had a girl, she would be one of the most powerful witches of her time. Lucas started to do work around the farm. He enjoyed working with his hands. Liz still worked part time at the archive office. Her artwork was now being sold in forty-eight out of fifty states and three foreign countries. Most of all the nightmares weren't as frequent. Liz contributed all of this to Lucas. He made her feel safe, but most of all it was because she wasn't alone anymore. He is her family; she wished she had asked him to stay sooner. Having his child was a huge honor and made her feel so complete.

Now with the truth being in print she felt free. It was so exhilarating to feel that way. Lucas would go out twice a week to make sure no threats were out there for Liz. Every night he would sit on the front porch for an hour. He would meditate as a protector. Since Katherine had died the few distant relatives remaining seemed happier. They had no animosity toward the Krimshaw family. Liz's skin no longer tingled when she passed a Blackthorne. The spell Katherine had cast was finally broken.

"Liz since you don't want to know until the birth. Can we at least talk baby names?"

"Sure," she grinned.

"I'd like to honor my grandmother for a girl's name."

"And a boy?"

She shrugged. Lucas tilted his head and looked at her in a knowing way. She started laughing. "I've known, just like I knew I was pregnant."

"So why wouldn't you let me say the gender a moment ago?"

"I didn't want to jinx it."

"You are such a superstitious witch."

"One of us has to be."

He kissed her forehead. "Your witch's sight is going to keep me on my toes isn't it."

"Yes sir."

He leaned down, kissed her, and then stopped. There was a kick at his touch. "Lucy." He spoke their child's name and there was another kick.

"She loves your voice almost as much as I do."

Joanna and Alec did book tour after book tour for a little over a year. The book was a New York Times bestseller for twenty weeks straight. Joanna was planning to send some of the royalty money to Liz, but Alec told her absolutely NOT, he explained that Liz wouldn't accept it.

Dec. 21 - Lucy Marie Briley-Maze was born to the proud parents Lucas and Liz Briley-Maze. When they had a boy, they agreed his name would be Marcus Krimshaw Briley-Maze, but it would be a few years before he entered the world. Lucy had raven hair with rich bronze skin. Lucas admired his daughter; she looked so much like her mother. The night Lucy had been born everyone had been asleep when the bedroom became very cold. Lucas jumped up to protect his wife and child, but Liz pulled him back in a reassuring way. A woman was standing by the bassinet, but Lucas knew she was a ghost.

"Hi grandmother," Liz said.

"I am so proud of you. Thank you."

The image of Lucy Krimshaw faded, and the room became warm again. Lucas was still in his protector mode.

"Would you please relax?" Liz asked.

"Is that becoming the norm?"

"Peace?"

"Ghosts?" he asked.

She laughed. "No that is not becoming the norm, peace is."

She was right he could feel the peace. He pulled her into his arms, and they drifted off to sleep. Lucy and Sherwan Krimshaw's souls were finally at rest. The wrongs had been righted in the best way possible, the truth. Liz's children would never live in fear of a Blackthorne. Liz deserved happiness and Lucas was honored to walk with her on this new journey. Liz and Lucas would train their children in all of their crafts, trades, and heritage. Liz was determined to ensure that spinners and seekers would not die out. Liz and Lucas would fly to New York once Lucy was six months old. Liz was excited to meet the woman who gave closure to the nightmares. She had a feeling they would be great friends, something that Liz was looking forward to. Lucas would work with Alec on hunting and fishing skills. The families could now be friends. Liz finally believed in happy-ever-after.

About the author

Sharon Barnes is a Native American author who lives in Rural, TN with her husband, children, grandchildren, and fur babies. She has received several awards for her poetry and was a top ten finalist in the Actions/Adventure category of the Claymore Award for her supernatural suspense work, Shanghai Sunset.

Sharon is an avid reader and loves to do research about other countries. She has a passion for other cultures, languages, folklores, myths, and legends. It amazes her how many countries and cultures have dragons in their legends. The supernatural world has always fascinated her and it is often incorporated in her stories. Rarely will you see Sharon without a cup of coffee, no matter the time; if she is awake, then coffee is close by.

Made in the USA
Columbia, SC
06 January 2025